REVENGE OF THE

Bubble Gum
Monster

by Marilyn D. Anderson

illustrated by Estella Hickman

Published by Willowisp Press, Inc.
801 94th Avenue North, St. Petersburg, Florida 33702

Printed in the United States of America

10 9 8 7 6 5 4 3 2

ISBN 0-87406-532-1

CONTENTS

1
Smile Spud Smile!

"Hey, how about a boa constrictor?" Jason Brown asked, leaping to his feet. "That would make a great mascot."

"Ick!" Beth said, making a face. "How about a unicorn? Everyone likes unicorns. They're so pretty and magical."

"No way," Joe griped. "I vote for gorillas."

"Now, class. Let's not argue," Miss Brings said. "Each of you should feel free to suggest anything you'd like as our new school mascot. We'll all vote on which idea we like best. Then the winning class will get to have a pizza party."

"Yeah!" all the kids screamed. Some of them even whistled or stomped their feet on the floor.

I looked over and saw that Shannon Smith was waving her hand in the air like crazy. Shannon always liked to be in the center of everything that was going on.

"I know what our mascot should be," she called out. "It should be a lion. And we could put Spud's picture on the posters. He's already got the perfect haircut for it."

"Oh, no," I groaned, resting my head in my hands. I knew that bringing Spud to school again wouldn't be such a good idea.

You see, Spud's my dog. He's usually a pretty good dog, but sometimes he gets into big trouble...like when I brought him to school for show and tell.

7

I had taught Spud to blow bubbles with bubble gum, but the kids at school didn't believe that he could do it. When I showed them, the kids got so excited that they gave Spud too much gum. He blew a bubble that grew and grew until it took over the whole classroom. And then it popped, making the biggest mess ever! The fire department had to come to our rescue! It was a total disaster.

That's how the kids at school got to know Spud. And that's why Spud has a terrible haircut. After the bubble gum mess, we had to take him to a special dog salon and they had to shave off big clumps of his hair just to get out all the pink goo. Spud really looks strange now.

"That might not be such a great idea,"
I spoke up. "Spud doesn't like the way
his fur looks. He'd never let you take
a picture of him."

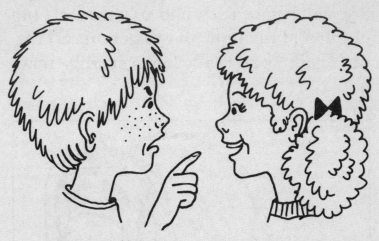

"Yes, he would," Shannon said.
"No, he wouldn't," I said.
"He would, too," she repeated.
We went back and forth until I
couldn't stand it anymore. I finally
agreed to let her try to take pictures of
Spud. And since Shannon always liked
to be in charge, she formed a "pick a
lion mascot" committee. The group
wanted to come to my house right after
school.

I was trapped. But at least I managed to talk my best friend Freddy into coming home with me. We ate cookies and watched a video until the committee arrived.

"Hi! Where's Spud?" asked Shannon as she barged into the room. She held onto a camera with one hand. Julie and Jenny, two other girls in our class, followed closely behind her.

I shrugged my shoulders. "He's probably behind the couch," I said.

Shannon leaned over and peeked beneath our old, tweed couch. "Here, Spudsy Wudsy," she called. "Come out and see the terrific lion's mane we've made for you."

Just then, I caught sight of Spud's tail disappearing behind the easy chair. So I nudged Shannon and pointed to where he was.

"Come on, Spudsy," she crooned. "Don't be shy. I think you look cute no matter what. I don't care if some of your hair was cut off."

I couldn't see Spud anymore, but I could hear him panting. Shannon reached into her pocket.

"Here's a special treat just for you, Spud," Shannon coaxed him. I leaned over to see what it was.

Smack in the middle of her palm sat a piece of bubble gum!

"Hey, don't give him that!" I yelled, lunging toward the piece of gum. But the girls pushed me away. Spud dived for the gum, too, and the girls tackled him.

Jenny put a mane made of yellow yarn around his neck while Shannon focused her camera. But before she could shoot her picture Spud hid his face.

They all looked so funny and frazzled that I started laughing.

"You poor fella," Julie said in an icky-sweet voice. "You think you don't look very handsome. But our beautiful mane makes you look just like a big lion."

Spud seemed to understand. His head popped up a little and all three girls patted him on the head. I saw that Spud was chewing his gum and a small bubble was forming in the corner of his mouth. He even seemed to smile a little.

Shannon shot me a look that said, "See, I knew he'd do it." Then she took the photo.

15

At school the next day, Spud's pictures were plastered everywhere. They all said: VOTE LIONS. Lots of kids pointed and giggled when they saw Spud. They seemed really excited by the idea.

But on Wednesday there were two new posters around school. One said, "Sting back with the yellow jackets. We'll soar to victory!" The other said, "Be a dragon and blaze a winning trail!"

Shannon got nervous about the new ideas and called an emergency meeting of our class.

"Okay, gang, I have a plan," she said. "Voting will be at the school carnival Saturday. So let's bring Spud with us. He'll get lots of attention. And then we'll win for sure."

"My mom and dad will never go for that," I spoke up. "They don't ever want to see the bubble gum monster again."

"We could write your parents a note," Shannon suggested. "We could promise to keep Spud away from bubble gum."

"Yeah," yelled the other kids.

I was sure my parents would turn us down. I figured there wasn't a chance in the world that Shannon could convince them. But I was wrong. She won again.

Spud Goes to the Carnival

2

The carnival is always held in the parking lot next to our school. There are games, contests, and prizes. It's usually a lot of fun.

As Spud and I headed to the carnival, I noticed that he actually looked kind of proud of his fake mane. Maybe Shannon had a good idea after all.

We got there before most of my friends did. I stood by the ticket booth and waited for them. Some kids were laughing and talking to the clowns. Others were eating popcorn and cotton candy. And there were a lot of cool games. There was even one where you could pay to have your friends thrown in a fake jail. But the best thing of all was the Bounce House. It looked like a huge plastic bag with people jumping inside it. And something like a giant vacuum cleaner pumped in air to keep it up.

Finally Freddy and the girls arrived. They brought a special, golden blanket for Spud to wear. They attached it to the mane with safety pins. On the blanket they'd written, "Votc Lions." I had to admit that Spud did look pretty neat.

We bought our tickets and went into the carnival. We stopped at the first game we came to. It was called The Wheel of Prizes, and winners got stuffed pandas. All you had to do was spin the wheel and get the slot that said winner. The man working at the booth wore a big, fake, red nose and a hat with a propeller on top.

Naturally, Shannon offered to go first. I wanted to see if she'd win, but at that moment two boys walked by and stared at Spud.

"Hey, look at the lion," one of them said.

"Yeah, he's pretty cool," said the other. "I'll vote for him."

Freddy nudged me and grinned. "Bringing Spud here was a good idea," he said.

Finally, Shannon spun The Wheel of Prizes. Spud's head went around and around as he watched it spin. All she won was a really crummy whistle. I snickered.

"Hey, Sam," someone else yelled. "You should take Spud down there." I looked over my shoulder and saw Joey Wagner. He was pointing in the direction of the fake jail.

"Why?" I asked.

"Because they're having a bubble gum-blowing contest," Joey explained, "and Spud could win it easily."

"No way!" I said. "There's no way that Spud will be in a bubble gum contest. I don't want the bubble gum monster to come back."

"But the judges would only give him one piece," Joey said. "He wouldn't be able to make a monster bubble."

I shook my head. "I'm not taking any chances," I said.

Each of us tried to win a panda bear. None of us did and we decided to move on.

The next game we came to was Cook the Chicken. People used a big hammer to hit a target. The target was part of a spring that threw a rubber chicken into the air. If the chicken landed in a cooking pot, you won a little red race car.

"This looks like fun. Let's try it," Freddy said, pointing to the silly chicken flying high into the air. It flopped off the edge of the pot and fell to the ground.

"Okay," I agreed.

"Ruff, ruff, ruff," Spud said, tugging on the leash and jumping at the rubber chicken.

"Stop, Spud, stop," I yelled. "Get down and be quiet."

Then three girls I didn't know very well stopped to talk.

"Isn't that the cute dog that blows bubbles?" one girl asked.

"Yep, it is," Shannon answered proudly. "We think that a lion would make a great school mascot and Spud is our lion. Can we count on your vote?"

"Yeah, sure," one girl said, pointing toward the fake jail. "But what about the bubble gum-blowing contest? Are you entering him in that, too?"

"No way!" I told her.

"Could we enter him?" a second girl asked.

"Yeah, he'd win for sure," the third girl said. "Please?"

"No!" I barked at them. Spud was my dog and there was no way I'd let him get into so much trouble again. Besides, my mom and dad would be furious— with both of us.

"What a grouch!" the first girl said and walked away. The others followed her.

28

Shannon glared at me. "Why did you have to yell at her?" she asked. "That wasn't very nice. And we need their votes, you know."

"Sorry," I mumbled.

Freddy picked up the hammer and
swung. A rubber chicken flew into the
air. Spud yelped and tried to chase after
it, but I wouldn't let him. The chicken
landed in the pot and Freddy screamed.

"I did it! I did it!" he sang, dancing around. The guy in charge of the game handed Freddy his prize.

"Way to go!" I said, slapping him on the shoulder. Then I saw that Jason and Robert were walking toward us.

"Hey, how's it going?" Jason asked us.

"I just won a car," Freddy announced.

"That's great," Robert said. "Would you guys like us to watch Spud for you?"

"No, thanks," I said. "I know what you're up to and Spud's not going to be in the bubble gum-blowing contest. And that's my final decision."

Jason and Robert looked at each other

sheepishly. "But why not?" Jason asked.

"You know what happens when Spud blows bubbles. There's always a huge disaster!" I said.

"But he's a cinch to win!" Jason said.

"NO!" I said, then stomped off. Then I walked to the next booth and watched as a woman did cartoon drawings of people's faces. Some of them were really funny.

Then I felt a tap on my shoulder. I turned around and saw three clowns standing over me. Each of them wore a sheriff's badge and a big grin.

"Okay, kids," the biggest clown said. "You're under arrest! Let's go! All of you follow me."

I gulped and gripped Spud's leash even tighter.

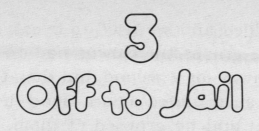

3
Off to Jail

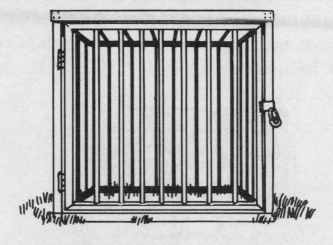

"Why? What did we do?" Jenny asked the tallest clown.

"Nothing," the clown said as we walked toward the jail cells. "We've been paid to take you to jail. It's all for fun, you know."

I saw Shannon narrow her eyes like she was thinking seriously about something. "Do you think we should make a run for it?" she whispered.

I nodded and we tried to break free from the grasps the clowns had on us. We got away for a second, but then they had us surrounded again. Spud didn't like that and he growled at them. For a minute, I thought the clowns might leave and forget about putting all of us in jail.

But no such luck.

And Jason and Robert seemed to appear out of nowhere.

"Need someone to watch Spud the lion for you?" Jason asked the clowns.

"Yeah," said the biggest one. "You paid us to put your friends in jail, but you didn't say that there'd be a dog. I don't want to get bitten."

Now I knew that some big trouble was brewing. If Jason was involved, problems were sure to follow.

"Okay, I'll take him," Jason said. "Spud's not crazy about grown-ups, but he loves kids."

The clown handed Spud's leash to Jason. Then they urged us toward the jail door.

"Give me back my dog!" I said to the clown that was holding on to me. "They're going to take him to the bubble gum-blowing contest. Then there's going to be the biggest mess you've ever seen. You've got to give me back my dog!"

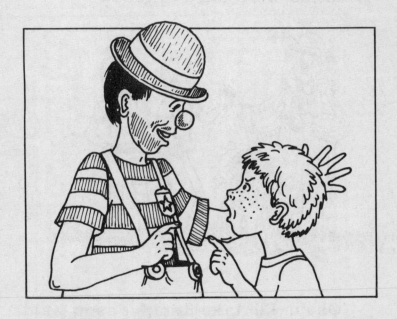

"It doesn't sound like a mess to me," the clown said. "It kind of sounds like fun. Let's go. Stop stalling. Be a good sport about this. A carnival is supposed to be fun."

The jail looked like a wooden cage. There were 10 prisoners inside. Outside of it, a bunch of clowns sat at tables drinking glasses of cola. Our clowns led us inside, shut the door, then walked over to join their friends.

I ran to look out the bars of the jail.
We were smack up against a popcorn
stand, but I could still see Spud's tail
as Jason led him away.

"Jason, come back," I yelled after
them. "You can't do this!"

"Jason, you're a major dweeb!"
Shannon yelled as loud as she could.

But then they were gone.

"I've got to get out," I told her. "We all know what could happen if Spud gets a hold of some bubble gum. Powee!"

"Yeah," she agreed.

I started banging my fists against the wooden bars. The other prisoners joined in, too.

I started to chant. "Let us out! Let us out! Let us out!" Everyone began yelling, too.

"Aw, quiet down," one of the clowns called back.

Luckily our principal, Mr. Todd, walked by right then. He stopped to talk to the clowns.

"Mr. Todd, help!" I screamed.

He glanced my way. Then he gave me a closer look. "Sam, is that you?" he asked.

"Yeah," I said. "I've got to get out of here. Jason took my dog Spud over to the big bubble-blowing contest."

"So?" Mr. Todd asked.

"It's with bubble gum. And they're going to enter Spud in the contest!" I explained.

I saw Mr. Todd's eyes grow as round as saucers. "Good grief! I remember what happened the last time that dog got hold of bubble gum!" he said. "How did all this happen?"

"It's a long story," I said. "But I've got to stop him before it's too late."

Mr. Todd looked at the biggest clown. "Let this boy out right now. It's an

emergency," he said.

The clown sprang into action. He fumbled with the door until another clown jumped in to help. Soon all the clowns were nervously trying to get the door open. When they finally did, the clowns bumped into each other and one fell down. If I hadn't been so scared of the bubble gum monster, the whole thing would've been super funny.

"This way," I yelled the second I was free. "They went this way." And I raced off with Mr. Todd right behind me.

The bubble gum-blowing contest was in a booth not far from the popcorn stand. Jason and Robert were leaning over the sales counter as we walked up. I didn't see Spud for a minute—until I looked beneath the counter. He had his head stuffed inside a big box that was marked Purple Power Bubble Gum.

"Jason, look what Spud's doing!" I screamed. "STOP HIM!!"

4 The Bubble Gum Monster Returns

Jason looked down. "Oh, no!" he cried.

"It's happening again!" I yelled.

We grabbed at Spud, but he was too quick for us. He leaped away and chomped on his gum. He started to blow bubbles, one right after the other.

"Oh, no! It might be too late!" Mr. Todd said, covering his eyes with his hands.

"Let's get behind Spud and try to tackle him," I suggested.

We hurried around to the back of the bubble gum booth. We watched helplessly as one of Spud's bubbles grew bigger and bigger.

I ran toward Spud then stopped. The bubble was huge. It picked up Jason and Robert and all the kids standing in line at the popcorn stand. I heard people scream. A woman pushing a baby carriage was slurped up, too.

"We've got to burst that bubble," Mr.
Todd said. "We need a long pole or
something to do it."

Before I could answer, I saw the lady
who painted faces try to run away. But
the funny outfit she wore got tangled
up around her feet. The pink monster
got her and all her paints. The huge
bubble turned every color of the rain-
bow. It was beautiful.

"How about a safety pin?" I asked. "There are some big ones holding Spud's lion blanket to his mane."

I scurried around Spud and his bubble.

"No, stop! Come back!" yelled Mr. Todd. "Don't go near the monster!"

I stood behind a pole and watched as the bubble gum monster gobbled up the clowns and their tables and chairs. It even swallowed the jail—with lots of kids inside. And still the bubble gum monster grew.

A cute basset hound puppy tried to run away from the bubble gum monster. But its little legs couldn't move fast enough. There was no escaping.

"It's got to be stopped," I called back. I was right behind Spud when the gum got the Cook the Chicken game. The man in charge threw himself on the ground. But it didn't help. He was picked up and carried away with his cooking pots and rubber chickens.

I took a deep breath and scurried up
behind Spud. I felt around his blanket
for a safety pin. With the bubble gum
monster just inches from me, I yanked
one of the pins out and held it over my
head.

"Take that, you bubble gum monster!" I cried out. And I jabbed at the
bubble until I heard a humongous POP!

A mighty BLAM! echoed through the air. Strings and globs and hunks of gum shot in all directions. We were free from the monster at last!

Rainbow-colored goo landed in trees, on cars, over houses. People and chairs and toys fell like rain. Everything was covered in wild colors.

"Help us!" people cried. "We're stuck in this slippery, goopy mess."

I wanted to help them, but a blanket of rainbow-colored gum had covered both Spud and me, too. Our feet wouldn't move and we had to fight just to keep our heads above it.

Then Mr. Todd picked up a crying baby. "Call the fire department," he yelled.

"Oh, no!" I said. "Not them again!"

The fire department had come to our rescue twice before and they were never going to believe the bubble gum monster was back.

5
The Bubble Gum Monster's Revenge

I heard sirens blaring a few minutes later. They got louder and louder. And then the fire department arrived.

The fire chief stopped at the edge of the gum and looked at the mess. He was the same guy who had been at our school a few weeks earlier. He knew what kind of messes the bubble gum monster left behind. And he didn't look happy.

"Why me?" the chief asked. "I can't believe that this could happen again!"

Mr. Todd ran to meet him. "I'm glad you're here!" he said. "Yes, the bubble gum monster came back to get us."

"Bubble gum?" asked a fireman I hadn't seen before. He started to laugh.

The fire chief gave him a mean look. "You're new here, Schwartz," he said. "But we don't laugh at bubble gum in this town."

The fireman's smile disappeared. "Sorry, Chief. It won't happen again."

The chief looked around at the mess. "Mr. Todd, we need something to suck up this stuff. Do you have any ideas?"

"I do," I said before Mr. Todd could answer. I hadn't meant to interrupt, but it had slipped out.

"Who said that?" the chief asked.

"Me, sir," I said.

He groaned. "Oh, it's you again," he said. "I should have known. You and your dog are nothing but trouble."

"That's true," Mr. Todd admitted, "but this time Sam really saved the day. He burst the bubble with a safety pin."

"Okay, kid. So what's your idea?" the chief asked.

"The Bounce House," I said more boldly. "My dad told me that it's like a vacuum cleaner turned backward. Maybe you could turn it around and suck up the gum."

"Well," he said, "your idea could work. I'll need some volunteers to move that Bounce House over here."

Lots of people offered to help. Soon they had the Bounce House turned around. One of the firemen held the hose connected to it. The house made a loud whoosh as it sucked up everything in sight. The colorful gum stretched in all directions and looked really scary. But finally the stuff began to move toward the hose.

As the people and things stuck in the gum soared by the firemen, they chopped everything loose. Spud and I were the last ones to be freed. Spud had lost even more fur and he looked sadder than ever.

"Gosh, I'm sorry," I told Mr. Todd. "I never wanted to bring Spud to the carnival."

"Then why did you?" he asked.

"Because my class wanted to win the mascot contest," I told him. "We dressed up Spud to look like a lion. Everything was fine at first. But then—even though I said no—Jason and Robert took Spud to the bubble gum-blowing contest. And, well, you know the rest."

Mr. Todd shook his head like he thought I was crazy.

Just then Jason and some other kids came running up. "Hey, Sam. We won!" he said. "We get the pizza party."

"Yeah, and that's not all," Shannon said. "Spud won the bubble-blowing contest, too! I just heard someone talking about it. They said they'd never seen anything like it before and that he deserved a special award."

"Oh, brother," the fire chief said.

"Well, I think Jason and Robert are going to be busy for a while," Mr. Todd said. "Maybe even too busy for pizza."

"Why?" Jason asked.

"Because you got Spud into trouble and now you're going to clean up the mess," he told them.

Jason and Robert looked at the ground. "Yes, sir," they both mumbled. The fire department handed them shovels and they began to scrape the goo off cars, buildings, and people. I put on rubber gloves to help them put the mess into trash cans.

A few minutes later I felt a tap on my shoulder. I saw that it was Shannon. She was wearing rubber gloves, too.

"I should help clean up, too, since bringing Spud to the carnival was my idea," she said, then grinned. "Oh, by the way, I called and told your mom and dad what happened."

"Were they mad?" I asked.

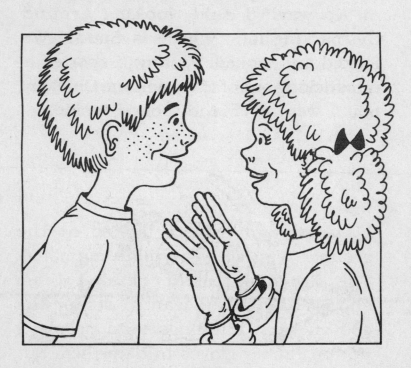

"Maybe a little. But I told them Spud's our mascot now. They laughed at that," Shannon said proudly.

"Our mascot's not Spud—it's a lion," I corrected her.

Shannon smiled. "But I think Spud should be our lion mascot all the time," she said, cleaning up the last pieces of gum. "Like at school parties and assemblies and stuff."

"No way!" I said, looking around the parking lot. "Where is Spud?" We looked and looked. Finally, I spotted a tail sticking out of the Cook the Chicken pot. I went over and looked inside.

"Spud, get out of there," I said. And then I saw what he was after—another piece of bubble gum! It was left over from the bubble-blowing contest.

I stuck my arms into the pot and tried to grab the gum. "No more bubble gum for you, Spud!" I yelled. "Not now! Not ever!"

About the Author

MARILYN D. ANDERSON grew up on a dairy farm in Minnesota. Her love of animals and her 20-plus years of training and showing horses are reflected in many of her books.

A former music teacher, Marilyn has taught choir and band for 17 years. She specializes in piano. She also stays busy training young horses, riding in dressage shows, giving piano lessons, and, of course, writing books. Marilyn and her husband live in Bedford, Indiana.

Revenge of the Bubble Gum Monster is the sequel to *The Bubble Gum Monster* and *The Bubble Gum Monster Strikes Again.*